Young Gabby Goose

RUTH MANNING-SANDERS

Young Gabby Goose, Pussy Bauldron and
Dog Towser and Lion all appear in this
collection of traditional stories selected
from countries as far afield as Zanzibar,
Russia and Finland.

Each tale is beautifully told with just the
right amount of humour, pathos and
suspense to make them ideal for reading
aloud or for young readers.

RUTH MANNING-SANDERS

Young Gabby Goose

Illustrated by James Hodgson

A Methuen Paperback

Also available in paperback and hardback

TORTOISE TALES
Ruth Manning-Sanders

First published in Great Britain 1975
by Methuen Children's Books Ltd
Methuen paperback edition first published 1976
by Methuen Children's Books Ltd
11 New Fetter Lane, London EC4P 4EE
Text copyright © 1975 Ruth Manning-Sanders
Illustrations copyright © 1975 Methuen Children's Books Ltd
Printed in Great Britain
by Cox & Wyman Ltd, London, Reading and Fakenham

ISBN 0 416 57540 4

Contents

1 · Young Gabby Goose and Mr Fickle Fox

Young Gabby Goose lived in the farmyard. The farmyard had a high wooden fence all round it. Young Gabby Goose looked through the fence at the fields and woods outside, and said to herself, 'How big and exciting the world is! If I were a little older, and my wings were a little stronger, I would fly over the fence and set off on my travels. Yes, I must practise flying!'

So every day, there was Young Gabby Goose going *hop hop hop* with her yellow feet, and *flap flap flap* with her white wings, teaching herself to fly. And she did soon manage

to fly up a little way, but never high enough to get over the fence.

So Gabby got angry and ran at the fence, hissing and calling it names. And the fence laughed and said:

'*Look low, look low,*
Instead of high;
Feet can go
Where wings can't fly.'

So then Gabby looked low. What did she see? She saw a hole in the fence, quite close to the ground. She stepped through the hole, and there she was – out in the big world.

'*Oh ho, oh ho!*
Which way shall I go?'

Gabby was turning her head this way, turning her head that way, craning her neck, looking out of one eye, looking out of the other eye, running a little here, running a little there, flapping her wings and dancing with excitement, when Mr Fickle Fox came creeping out of the wood.

Mr Fickle Fox was hungry. He had been stalking some young pigeons. But Mother Pigeon had called the young ones back into their nest at the top of a tree.

Mr Fickle Fox couldn't climb the tree. So he thought that such things as trees shouldn't exist. But now here was Young Gabby Goose; and if Mr Fickle Fox couldn't climb trees, neither could Gabby. So he ran to where Gabby was staring about her, and said, 'Well met, Gabby my dear! Well met, my breakfast!'

'Oh *no*!' said Gabby, '*not* your breakfast, just when I was having a look at the big world! Oh, please do let me have one last look! And if you could just let me have one last dance at the same time, I think I could die happily!'

'Well,' said Mr Fickle Fox, 'I'm a good-natured sort of fellow. Take your last look, and have your last dance, but you mustn't be long about it, because my mouth's watering and my stomach's grumbling, and I really must eat *something*.'

'Oh, I promise you I won't be long!' said Gabby. And she began to dance, flapping her wings and wagging her head, and turning her long neck this way and that way. *Hop hop, flap flap! Hop hop, flap flap!* She looked so silly that Mr Fickle Fox burst out laughing.

'Ha ha! Ha ha!' laughed Mr Fickle Fox. 'This is as good as a play! This sets an edge to my appetite! Go it, Gabby my love, go it!'

Mr Fickle Fox laughed till the tears streamed out of his eyes, and he couldn't see anything. So he turned his head to wipe his eyes with his tail. But Gabby had been dancing back towards the hole in the fence; and while Mr Fickle Fox was wiping his eyes, she scrambled through the hole into the farmyard.

'Oh, you vile deceiver!' There was Mr Fickle Fox scrambling through the hole after her; and there was Gabby rushing with long strides across the farmyard and screaming at the top of her voice, 'The fox! The fox! *Help! Help! Help!*'

'*Bow, wow wow wow!*' Out from the farm-house door rushed Bevis the big hound, and Blackie the terrier, and Blinkie the little dachshund with his crooked legs. *Bow, wow*

wow, gr-gr-gr! The dogs rushed, Gabby flapped her wings; she gave a leap and flew, yes, she *flew* right over the heads of the dogs and into the barn. Ah ha! The game's up, Mr Fickle Fox. You might fight one dog, but you can't fight three. The dogs pounced, Mr Fickle Fox turned and fled.

He fled back through the hole in the fence, he fled back into the wood, he fled into his lair under an oak tree; and the dogs stood round the tree, barking till the wood echoed.

And at the farm Young Gabby Goose sat in the barn gulping and wheezing.

'The world is a very dangerous place,' said Young Gabby. 'If I should live for a hundred years I wouldn't go out into the world again. No no, never again!'

2 · Hello, House!

As Lion was walking through the wood he passed under a tree where some bees had a nest. The bees were flying about collecting honey, and one of them settled on Lion's nose. Lion put up a paw to knock the bee off his nose, and the bee was frightened and stung him. Then it flew away.

Lion danced with pain and roared with rage.

'You miserable bees,' he roared, 'I'll fetch a burning brand, I'll set fire to your tree, I'll burn your nest and your grubs and your honey and everything!'

The bees said, 'Oh, oh, *please* don't do

that, Lion! We're very sorry – it was all a mistake!'

And they gave Lion a honeycomb.

Lion was pleased. He put the honeycomb down under the tree, and said, 'I'll fetch it on my way home.'

Then he went farther into the wood.

Well, Lion hadn't been gone long when Mr and Mrs Hare came skipping by.

'Oh ho! See what's here!' cried Hare. 'A breakfast fit for kings and queens! A whole honeycomb! Eat up, my dear, eat up!'

Then Mr and Mrs Hare ate up the whole honeycomb, and skipped off, licking their lips and laughing.

By and by back comes Lion.

'What, what, where's my honeycomb?'

'Oh Lion,' said the bees, 'Mr and Mrs Hare came by, and they ate it all up.'

'They did, did they?' roared Lion. 'Well, that's the last meal *they*'ll ever eat. Where's their house? Tell me, someone, so that I may go and kill them!'

The bees said they didn't know where Hare's house was. Lion raged off. He was

asking everyone he met where Mr and Mrs Hare lived. Nobody wanted to tell him; but he frightened them so that at last little Master Weasel said, 'They live over there on the top of that hill.'

Then off rushed little Master Weasel as

fast as he could to warn Mr and Mrs Hare that Lion was coming to kill them.

So Mr and Mrs Hare went out of their house, and ran off quite a long way, and hid under some bushes.

They kept peeping out from under the bushes; and by and by they saw Lion go stamping past. They waited a while, and then Hare said to Mrs Hare, 'You stay here, my dear.' And he crept softly away, following the tracks of Lion's feet in the grass.

The tracks led right up to Hare's house, and there they stopped. And Hare said to himself, 'Oh ho! Lion's inside!' And he went to stand at a little distance and called out, 'Hello, House! Hello, House!'

Then he listened.

No answer.

Lion, hidden behind the closed door, was licking his lips. 'I'll have him in a minute or two,' Lion was thinking.

Hare called again, 'Hello, House!'

No answer.

Hare said, 'This is very strange! Every day when I come home, if I say, "Hello, House," and there's nobody at home, the house answers, "Hello, Hare!" But today it says nothing. I think there must be someone inside it!'

Lion, listening inside the closed door, thought, 'If that's the case, I ought to have answered.'

'Perhaps my house is getting deaf,' said Hare, 'I must shout louder.' Then he bawled at the top of his voice, *'Hello, House!'*

And this time Lion shouted back, 'Hello, Hare!'

'Oh ho, Lion!' called Hare. 'Are you there, waiting to eat me? Ha ha! Lion! When did you ever hear of a house talking?' And he scuttled off and hid again under the bushes.

Lion came out of the house. He was

searching everywhere for Hare, but he couldn't find him. He was searching till he got tired. So then he went home. And to

everyone he met, he said, 'If you should see that miserable little thief of a Hare, you can tell him that I despise him. Eat him? Not I! Bah! the very thought of him makes me feel sick!'

3 · Clever Sparrow

A hungry fox sat under an oak tree; and up in the tree a gay little sparrow was merrily chirping.

The sparrow cocked her head on one side; she looked down through the branches of the oak tree and saw the fox.

'Brother Fox,' said she, 'why do you sit there so solemn, so solemn, as if you were thinking of a sermon to preach on Sunday?'

And the fox answered, 'When a body is as hungry as I am, Sister Sparrow, a body doesn't think about sermons. I'm thinking about my empty stomach, and how to fill it.'

Little Sister Sparrow said, 'Cheer up! Cheer up! I'll soon fill your stomach for you. I see a boy coming this way with a basket under his arm. Do you know what he is carrying in that basket, Brother Fox? He is carrying dinner for his father, the wood-cutter, who is working deep in the forest. I think there is meat in that basket, Brother Fox, and a dumpling or two, and maybe

some cakes. Now stay quietly where you are, and I will set to work. You shall have the meat and dumplings, and maybe the cake, Brother Fox; and I will have the crumbs!'

Then Little Sister Sparrow flew down

from the tree. Now she was fluttering along the path in front of the boy with the basket. She was trailing one wing as if she had broken it. When the boy saw her, he put down the basket he was carrying, and hurried after her.

Sister Sparrow hopped, hopped, hopped, trailing her wing. She hopped as quickly as she could, but still she trailed that wing. Every now and then the boy gave a pounce and tried to catch her; but she fluttered up just out of his reach, and came down a little farther on, still trailing her wing. She hopped ever deeper into the forest, right out of sight of the basket; and still the boy followed her.

Now's your chance, Brother Fox! Brother Fox jumped up, he ran to the basket; he gave that basket one snap with his strong white teeth, and turned it upside down. Out tumbled the meat, out tumbled the dumplings, out tumbled some cheese, out tumbled half a currant cake. Meat, dumplings, cheese and cake – Brother Fox gobbled up the lot. Then he went back to sit under the oak tree. He was licking his lips and smiling.

Little Sister Sparrow flew to the top of a tree. The boy stared up at her.

'Oh, you little cheat, there's nothing the matter with *your* wing!'

Then he remembered his father's dinner and ran back to where he had left the basket. See there! The basket upside down, all the food gone! Oh me, now he'll catch it! He snatched up the basket and hurried home, to fetch another dinner for his father.

Little Sister Sparrow went to pick up the crumbs. Then she came to where Brother Fox sat smiling under the oak tree.

'Well, brother, how do you find yourself? Is your stomach full?'

'My stomach is quite full, and thank you

for that, Sister Sparrow! Do you know what I should like now?'

'What would you like, Brother Fox?'

'Little Sister Sparrow, I should like a good laugh.'

'Well then, follow me, Brother Fox, and you shall have a good laugh.'

So Brother Fox got up and followed Little Sister Sparrow. She led him to a barn where two men with bald heads – Bald Headed Billy, and Bald Headed Ben – were threshing corn.

'Go round to the back of the barn, Brother Fox,' said Little Sister Sparrow. 'Climb up on to the roof of the barn, and you'll find a hole in it. Creep through the hole and look down through the rafters. Then you shall laugh.'

So round to the back of the barn went Brother Fox, got through the hole in the roof, stretched himself out on the rafters, and looked down. What did he see? He saw

Bald Headed Billy and Bald Headed Ben threshing away at the corn with their flails. Was he supposed to laugh at that? No, it didn't seem to him at all funny.

But, oh – see now! Little Sister Sparrow has flown into the barn. *Hipperty-hop!* Now she sits perched on the head of Bald Headed Billy. And – see now! Bald Headed Ben swings his flail to knock Little Sister Sparrow off Bald Headed Billy's head. But Little Sister Sparrow flies up and away; and – *whop!* – down comes the flail on Bald Headed Billy's head.

'Hey! Hey! What you mean by that?' Bald Headed Billy is furious; he swings *his* flail – *whop!* Down comes the flail on Bald Headed Ben's head. Oh! Ah! Bald Headed Ben is furious in his turn; he swings his flail again, *whop!* And if the first blow was kindly meant, this second blow isn't. Now they are at it hammer and tongs, both furious, both shouting, jumping round the barn, and hitting away at each other, *whop whop whop!*

Brother Fox, looking down through the rafters, bursts out laughing. He laughs and laughs, he loses his balance, slips off one of the rafters, makes a grab – no, can't hold on, down he comes in a smother of straw and rubbish, right on top of the two Bald Heads.

'Oh! Oh! Oh! What's this? Now we've raised the Devil with our shouting and swearing, and here he comes jumping down to catch us!'

Bald Headed Billy and Bald Headed Ben are scared out of their wits, they fling down their flails and rush out of the barn, shouting, 'The Devil! The Devil is after us!'

They run, run, and don't stop running till they get home.

Brother Fox is laughing. Little Sister Sparrow is laughing. Brother Fox laughs till the tears stream down his face. He wipes his eyes with his tail and says, 'Little Sister Sparrow, what a one you are! Now you and I must be friends to the end of our lives.'

'So we shall be,' said Little Sister Sparrow.

And so they were.

4 · Koko and the waterfall

A little boy, called Koko, went out to play by a waterfall, and he found a green frog under a willow root. He took the frog home to show to his mother.

His mother was standing in the doorway. She said, 'The birds are in the garden eating my peas. Quick, Koko, run and chase them off.'

Koko gave the green frog to his mother and ran into the garden to chase off the birds. His mother put Koko's frog down outside the door, and it hopped away.

By and by Koko came in again, and when he found his frog was gone, he cried

out, 'Mother, give me back my frog, my
green frog that I found under the willow
root by the waterfall, under the willow root!'

But Koko's mother couldn't give him
back his frog, so she gave him a piece of cake
to comfort him. Koko went off with the
cake; he put it down on a tree stump, and
the white ants came and ate it up. Then
Koko cried out, 'White ants, give me back
my cake, my cake that my mother gave me,
because she lost my frog, my green frog that
I found under the willow root by the waterfall, under the willow root!'

Then the white ants made a little clay pot for Koko. Koko carried the little clay pot to the waterfall, to fill it with water. But the whirlpool carried the pot away, and broke it, and Koko cried out, 'Whirlpool, give me back my pot, my clay pot that the white ants made for me, because they ate the cake that my mother gave me, because she lost my frog, my green frog that I found under the willow root by the waterfall, under the willow root!'

Then the whirlpool gave Koko a little fish; but a hawk flew down and snatched the fish from him and swallowed it. And Koko cried out, 'Hawk, give me my fish again, my fish that the whirlpool gave me, because the whirlpool broke my little pot that the white ants gave me, because the white ants ate the cake that my mother gave me, because she lost my frog, my green frog that I found under the willow root by the waterfall, under the willow root!'

Then the hawk let a feather fall down for Koko. But a puff of wind carried the feather away. And Koko called out, 'Wind, give me back my feather, my feather that the hawk gave me, because the hawk ate my fish that the whirlpool gave me, because the whirlpool broke my little pot that the white ants gave me, because the white ants ate the cake that my mother gave me, because she lost my frog, my green frog that I caught myself, under the willow root by the waterfall, under the willow root.'

Then the wind went into the cherry tree and tossed down a lot of cherries for Koko; but a monkey came running and ate them all. And Koko cried out, 'Monkey, give me my cherries again, my cherries that the wind tossed down to me, because the wind carried away my feather, my feather that the hawk gave me, because the hawk ate my little fish, my little fish that the whirlpool gave me, because the whirlpool broke my little pot, my little pot that the white ants made for me, because the white ants ate my cake, my cake that my mother gave me, because my mother lost my frog, my green

frog that I found myself under the willow root by the waterfall, under the willow root.'

But the monkey said, 'I have nothing to give you except myself.'

So Koko took the monkey by the hand, and they walked home together.

5 · Dove, Fox and Raven

A dove built her nest in a high tree, and in the nest she laid three eggs. And a fox came along with an axe he had made out of clay. He stood under the tree and called up, 'Dove, I am going to chop down this tree to make myself snow-shoes.'

Dove said, 'Oh, oh, don't do that! I have my nest up here with three eggs in it!'

Fox said, 'Throw me down an egg and I'll spare the tree.'

Dove threw down an egg. Fox caught it and swallowed it.

Next day Fox came again. 'Dove, throw me another egg, or I'll chop down the tree.'

So Dove threw down another egg, and Fox swallowed it and went away.

On the thid day Fox came again. 'Dove, are you going to throw me another egg, or shall I chop down the tree?'

Dove threw down her third and last egg. And when Fox had swallowed it he went away.

And Dove sat and mourned on her empty nest.

Then Raven came along and said, 'Dove, why do you mourn?'

Dove told him and Raven said, 'Haven't

we birds got wings? If Fox cuts down this tree you can fly to another one, and build a new nest and lay more eggs. If Fox comes again, you tell him what I've said.'

So then Dove cheered up. And when, on the next day, Fox came again, Dove said, 'Chop away! I'm taking Raven's advice. If you chop down this tree, I shall fly to another one, and build a new nest, and lay more eggs.'

Fox was angry. He gave the tree a blow with his clay axe. But the axe broke. Dove laughed. Fox went away muttering, 'Raven has spoiled my little game. Now I will kill Raven!'

So he lay down and pretended to be dead. Raven saw him, and came hopping, hopping, very cautiously. He said, 'Is Fox dead? No, I don't think he is! Dead foxes move an ear.'

So Fox moved an ear, and Raven knew he was alive and flew away.

Next day Fox pretended to be dead again, and Raven came hopping. 'Can Fox be dead? Dead foxes twitch their tails.'

So Fox twitched his tail, and Raven knew he was alive and flew away.

Next day Fox pretended to be dead for the third time. Raven came hopping, hopping. 'Can Fox be dead? Dead foxes wink their eyes.'

But Fox didn't wink his eyes. He kept them shut tight.

So then Raven hopped quite close, and Fox gave a jump and caught him.

'Oh me!' whimpered Raven. 'Now I know that my grandad was a prophet. He said, "One day a fox will catch you, and he will carry you to the top of a steep rocky cliff and throw you down; and you will be broken in pieces, here a little leg, and there a little neck, and there a little wing – and the fox will gobble up every little bit."'

Fox thought that was a splendid idea – it would serve Raven right! So he carried Raven in his mouth up to the top of a steep rocky cliff and threw him down.

'Ha! Ha!' Raven spread his wings and flew away. 'Pick up the pieces, friend Fox! Pick up the pieces!'

Fox said, 'If there's one thing I dislike more than another it's deceit. Raven is a most deceitful bird!'

And he went into his lair and sulked.

6 · Baby Brother and the geese

Little Girl had a baby brother. And one day Little Girl's mother put Baby Brother in his cradle, in the parlour, and said to Little Girl, 'Your father and I are going to market. You stay in the parlour and look after Baby Brother. When we come back we will bring you – oh, such a pretty little dress.'

Then Little Girl's mother and father got into the pony cart and drove away.

Little Girl sat on the floor in the parlour. The sun was shining through the window. It looked so pretty outside, with the flowers bright in the sun, and the birds hopping among the bushes. Little Girl forgot that she had been told to stay in the parlour. Baby Brother was asleep. She lifted him from his cradle, carried him out, and laid him down on the grass under the window.

Little Girl hopped and skipped, picked some flowers, wandered here, wandered there. She was going farther and farther away from Baby Brother, who lay sleeping on the grass under the parlour window. Then came a flock of wild geese. They snatched up Baby Brother, and carried him off.

Little Girl came skipping back. Oh me, no Baby Brother! She burst into tears, she ran about looking. She heard the whistle of wings. She looked up, she saw the wild geese flying away with Baby Brother. 'Oh, what shall I do?'

She began to run after the wild geese; they were flying away, over the houses, over the fields. They disappeared behind the dark forest.

Little Girl ran on and on. She came to a little oven full of cakes.

'Little Oven, little Oven, tell me, where have the wild geese gone?'

Little Oven said, 'My cakes are going to burn, take them out, and then I will tell you.'

Little Girl took the cakes out of the oven, and laid them on the ground. Little Oven said, 'The geese flew that way, over to the left.'

Little Girl ran to the left. She didn't see the wild geese. She came to an apple tree with its branches all bowed down under its weight of fruit.

'Little Apple Tree, little Apple Tree, tell me, which way have the wild geese gone?'

The tree said, 'I am tired, tired. Pick my apples that I may lift up my branches again; then I will tell you.'

Little Girl climbed up among the branches; she picked all the apples, and put them in a pile on the ground. Then the apple tree lifted up its branches and said, 'The wild geese have flown to the right, they have carried Baby Brother to the house of Old Witch Bony Leg.'

Little Girl ran on to the right. She came to the house of Old Witch Bony Leg. She peeped through the window. She saw Old Witch Bony Leg asleep by the stove, and Baby Brother sitting on the table, playing with a golden ball.

Little Girl tiptoed into the house. She snatched up Baby Brother and ran out. She ran, ran. Old Witch Bony Leg woke up, looked round – no Baby Brother! Old Witch Bony Leg called to her flock of geese, 'After them, after them, my geese! Bring back Baby Brother, bring Little Girl as well!'

Little Girl was running, running, with Baby Brother in her arms. The wild geese were flying, flying; they were swooping low, they were catching up with Little Girl. Oh, oh, what to do? Little Girl came to the apple tree:

> *'Apple Tree, Apple Tree, hide us,*
> *So that the geese shan't find us!'*

The apple tree let down its branches. It hid Little Girl and Baby Brother under its green leaves. The geese didn't see anybody there. They flew on.

'Thank you, thank you, Apple Tree!'

Little Girl came out from under the green leaves. She ran on. The geese were circling round and round in the air; they saw Little Girl running, they turned and flew after her.

Little Girl came to the oven:

'Oven, Oven, hide us,
So that the geese shan't find us!'

The oven said, 'I'm cooled down nicely now; so open my door and creep inside.'

Little Girl, with Baby Brother in her arms, crept into the oven. The geese were swooping round. But they couldn't see Little Girl, they couldn't see Baby Brother.

They were cackling and scolding. 'Why should we fly any farther? No, we won't fly any farther!'

So they turned and flew back to Old Witch Bony Leg.

The oven said to Little Girl, 'You can come out now. The geese have gone away.'

Little Girl opened the oven door and came out. 'Thank you, thank you, dear Oven!'

Now she was safe; she ran on with Baby Brother in her arms; she came home. And there were her mother and her father returned from market, and just getting out of the pony cart.

Yes, they had brought Little Girl such a pretty little dress; they had brought Baby Brother a silver rattle.

7 · Pussy Bauldron and Dog Towser

One morning Pussy Bauldron found three pennies in the grass by the side of the road.

'Oh, what luck!' said Pussy Bauldron. 'With these pennies I can set up in business! But what business? I know – tailoring!'

Then on she scampered into town and bought a pennyworth of pins and needles, a penny reel of cotton, and a penny thimble.

'I ought to have a tape-measure too,' said Pussy Bauldron. 'But never mind – I can take my measurements with a piece of string.'

So off with her home again, and wrote out a notice. It said:

Madame P. B. Bauldron.
Ladies' and Gentlemen's Tailoring.
All orders promptly and neatly executed.

The notice was rather untidy because Pussy Bauldron wasn't very handy with a pen; there were some smears of ink here and there. But it was plain enough to read, and that was all that mattered. So she hung the notice on her garden gate, and went back into the house. She laid the reel of cotton,

and the pins and needles and the thimble on the parlour table, then she sat down to wait for customers.

Rat-tat-tat! Someone knocking on her front door.

Pussy Bauldron opened the door, and in walked Dog Towser, carrying a red and green striped rug.

'Good morning, Mrs Bauldron!'

'Good morning to you, Mr Towser!'

'There's a nip in the air today, Mrs Bauldron.'

'So there is, Mr Towser.'

'Winter will soon be upon us, Mrs Bauldron.'

'So it will, Mr Towser.'

'Well, since that is so, Mrs Bauldron, I should like you to make me a nice warm overcoat out of this rug.'

'I shall be pleased to do so, Mr Towser. And now I'll just take your measurements.'

Pussy Bauldron laid a piece of string along Dog Towser's back from neck to tail, and made a knot in the string. Then she passed the string round Dog Towser's body, and made another knot in it. She felt very businesslike.

'Thank you, that will be all, Mr Towser,' she said.

'And when shall I call for the coat, Mrs Bauldron?'

'Let us say this day week, Mr Towser.'

'Right.' Dog Towser hung the red and green striped rug over a chair-back, and went away.

Pussy Bauldron stood and looked at the rug. 'Dear me,' she said to herself, 'what does one do first . . .? Oh, of course, one cuts the thing out!'

Pussy Bauldron hadn't any scissors, so she fetched the garden shears. 'There must be holes for his legs to come through,' she said.

Chip, chop! Holes, certainly: but somehow they didn't seem to be in the right places. So she cut more holes. Then she pinned the edges of the rug together, and draped it over herself with her legs through the holes.

'It isn't much like an overcoat yet,' she said. 'What's the matter with it? Oh, I know, it's too floppy. I must cut it into shape.'

So Pussy Bauldron took up the shears

again, and set to work. *Chip, chop! Chip, chop!*
Now the floor was strewn with pieces of rug,
but what was left on the table looked less
like an overcoat than ever. Pussy Bauldron
got angry with it. She tossed it into a cupboard and slammed the cupboard door on
it. Then she gathered up the pieces from the
floor and burned them in her stove. They
smelled horrid. Pussy Bauldron flung open
the front door and went out into the
garden.

'Bother the overcoat!' she said. 'I shan't
make it.'

In a week there was Dog Towser again.

'Good morning, Mrs Bauldron. I've
called for my overcoat.'

'Oh dear, Mr Towser, I haven't been
able to make you an overcoat. The stuff
wasn't suitable. What about a nice pair of
trousers?'

Dog Towser was disappointed. But he
was a good-tempered fellow. So he said,

'Very well, Mrs Bauldron. And when will the trousers be ready?'

'Say this day week, Mr Towser.'

'Good. I'll call for them in a week, Mrs Bauldron.'

Dog Towser went away. Pussy Bauldron took the remains of the rug out of the cupboard and laid it on the table. *Chip, chop! Chip, chop!* The shears were very stiff, they made Pussy Bauldron's paws ache. And the thing she managed to cut out at last wasn't a bit like a pair of trousers.

'Oh bother you!' said Pussy Bauldron, and tossed the thing back into the cupboard.

In a week, there was Dog Towser knocking at the door. 'Good Morning, Mrs Bauldron. I've come for my trousers.'

'Oh Mr Towser, I couldn't make a pair of trousers out of that stuff. It's *much* too thick.'

'Well, Mrs Bauldron, what *can* you make me?'

'A nice warm waistcoat, Mr Towser. You can call for it this day week.'

'Very well, Mrs Bauldron, if that's the best you can do,' sighed Dog Towser. And he went away.

A week went by. But Pussy Bauldron could no more make a waistcoat than she could make an overcoat or a pair of trousers. She chopped away with the shears and all that happened was that the piece of rug that was left got smaller and smaller. There wasn't enough now for a waistcoat, even if Pussy Bauldron had known how to make it.

'He'll have to do with a cap,' she said. 'A nice cap with ear flaps. But then – how does one make a cap? I'm tired out, that's what I am!' and she curled up on what remained of the rug, and went to sleep.

In a week Dog Towser came for his waistcoat. Pussy Bauldron had tidied up the parlour, but there wasn't any sign of the waistcoat. 'I've been thinking,' said she. 'What you really need, Mr Towser, is a nice cosy cap with ear flaps to keep out the cold. Call a week today, and the cap will be ready.'

'Oh Mrs Bauldron, Mrs Bauldron!' said Dog Towser. 'I usually have my temper well under control. But now I can feel it rising – you mustn't try me too far!'

'You don't mean to say that you would insult a lady, Mr Towser?'

'Oh no, certainly not, Mrs Bauldron. Very well – this day week.'

And Dog Towser went away.

Pussy Bauldron opened the cupboard door and gazed thoughtfully at the fragments of the red and green rug. 'Why did I say a cap with ear flaps?' she sighed. 'Well, I suppose I must make him *something*. But what? Ah, I have it! A pretty tea cosy!' And she picked up two pieces of the rug and pinned them together.

'Now that does really look like a tea cosy,' she said. 'I think Dog Towser will be please with that!'

But when Dog Towser called again, he wasn't a bit pleased. 'Well really, Mrs Bauldron, what do I want with a tea cosy?' he growled. 'You ought to know that I never drink tea! But I'll take back what's left of the rug, if you please, Mrs Bauldron. I can at least wrap it round me when the snow falls.'

Pussy Bauldron knew that there wasn't enough left of his rug to wrap up a mouse. So she told Dog Towser to call again that day week, and she would then have something really useful ready for him.

'Well, see that you do,' grunted Dog Towser. And he went away.

Next week, there he was again, knocking at the door. Pussy Bauldron let him in. She was all smiles. She opened the cupboard door and brought out something very small, tacked round with large stitches and tied at the neck with string.

'What's this?' said Dog Towser.

'It's a purse,' said Pussy Bauldron. 'A purse to put your money in. Then you can go to town and buy yourself everything you need: a warm overcoat, a pair of trousers, a waistcoat, a cap with ear flaps and. . . .'

'*Gr-rr-rr-rr!*' The hackles rose along Dog Towser's back. He lifted his lip, showed all his white teeth, and made a snap at Pussy Bauldron. Pussy Bauldron put out her claws, scratched Dog Towser's nose, turned and galloped away through the open door. Dog Towser raced after her, barking madly. Pussy Bauldron ran for her life, she came to a tree, and clambered up into it.

There was Dog Towser now, galloping round and round the tree, and barking, barking. And there was Pussy Bauldron crouched on a branch and glaring down at him. She was growling and meowling and spitting, and every hair on her back was standing on end.

'You can't reach me,' she spat out. 'You'd best go home.'

Well, Dog Towser knew he couldn't reach her; and in the end he did go home.

But now every time he sees Pussy Bauldron he rushes at her, barking furiously. And Pussy Bauldron spits, backs away, turns and runs for her life, to clamber up on to some tree or wall, where Dog Towser can't reach her. Once they were friends, now they are enemies. And all because Pussy Bauldron found three pennies in the grass by the side of the road.

8 · The glove

A man had a field on the edge of a wood, and the field was full of thorn bushes. The man said to himself, 'I will cut down those thorn bushes and make a garden.' He put on a pair of thick gloves so that the thorns shouldn't prick his hands, took his axe, and went to cut down the bushes.

He chopped, chopped, chopped; he cut down all the thorn bushes; he piled them up tidily on the edge of the wood. Then he took off his gloves, laid down his axe, and went off to town to buy some flower seeds. He didn't notice that he had dropped one of his gloves in the field, because he was

thinking so much of the garden he was
going to make.

And the glove lay in the field until the
evening.

Then came little Nibbling Mouse, and
crept into the glove.

'Now I have a cosy house,' said little Nibbling Mouse.

Then came little Croaking Frog and said,
'Who is in this glove?'

'Little Nibbling Mouse. And who are
you?'

'I am little Croaking Frog. Let me come
in too!'

'Come then!'

So little Croaking Frog crept into the glove. Now there were two of them.

Then came little Hopping Hare, and said, 'Who is in this glove?'

'Little Nibbling Mouse and little Croaking Frog. And who are you?'

'I am little Hopping Hare. Let me come in too!'

'Come then!'

So little Hopping Hare crept into the glove, and now there were three of them.

Then came Sister Fox running and said, 'Who is in this glove?'

'Little Nibbling Mouse, little Croaking Frog, little Hopping Hare. And who are you?'

'I am Sister Fox. Let me come in too!'

'Oh well, come!'

So Sister Fox crept into the glove, and now there were four of them.

Then came big Brother Wolf galloping, and said, 'Who is in this glove?'

'Little Nibbling Mouse, little Croaking Frog, little Hopping Hare, and Sister Fox. Who are you?'

'I am big Brother Wolf. Let me come in too.'

'Come then!'

So big Brother Wolf crept into the glove; and now there were five of them.

Then came Wild Boar running.

Grumph, grumph, grumph! 'Who is in this glove?'

'Little Nibbling Mouse, little Croaking Frog, little Hopping Hare, little Sister Fox, big Brother Wolf – and who are you?'

'I am Wild Boar with the long tusks. Let me come in too.'

'Oh, this is frightful! Each one who comes wants to get into the glove! Where will you find room?'

'I'll soon find room – only let me come in.'

'Well, what can we do with you? Come in!'

So Wild Boar with the long tusks crept into the glove. Now there were six of them. And they were so crowded that nobody could move.

Then in the wood behind the field the tree branches crashed together; and out of the wood great Brother Bear came lumbering.

Great Brother Bear looked at the glove and roared, 'Who is in here?'

'Little Nibbling Mouse, little Croaking Frog, little Hopping Hare, little Sister Fox, big Brother Wolf, Wild Boar with the long tusks – and who are you?'

'I am great Brother Bear. Let me come in too.'

'What shall we do with you in here, when we're packed so tight we can scarcely breathe?'

'You must make room somehow.' And

Great Brother Bear crept into the glove.

Now there were seven of them. Glove thought every moment that it was going to split!

'I can't endure it,' said glove. 'I can't endure it!'

'You must endure it,' said they.

And they all lay still.

Well, the man had bought his flower seeds and come home from market. Then he noticed that one of his gloves was missing. So he went to the field to look for it; and he took big Dog Faithful with him.

'Faithful, big Dog Faithful, find my glove!'

Big Dog Faithful ran ahead. *Sniff sniff sniff!* He found the glove lying beside the pile of thorn bushes. The glove was heaving and shuddering.

Wow wow wow! Big Dog Faithful jumped round the glove and barked till the wood echoed.

Then out of the glove rushed little Nibbling Mouse, little Croaking Frog, little Hopping Hare, Sister Fox, Brother Wolf, Wild Boar with the long tusks, and great Brother Bear. They were all so frightened that they fled away into the wood.

Big Dog Faithful took the glove in his white teeth, gave it a shake, and carried it to the man.

The man put the glove in his pocket and turned to go home. And the glove said, 'Don't you go and drop me again, my fine fellow. It's all very well housing your fingers; but when it comes to housing all those animals – well, it's like swallowing too much pudding!'

9 · The kitten and the knitting-needles

A poor woman had a little cottage, and a little shed, and a little nanny-goat, and two little children.

Now it was winter-time, very cold, and the snow lay thick on the ground. The woman got up early, while it was still dark, lit the kitchen fire, took a lantern, and went into the shed to milk the nanny-goat. Then she gave the nanny-goat some hay, carried the pail full of milk into the kitchen, and made some porridge.

While the porridge was cooking, she washed and dressed the children. Then she gave them each a bowl full of porridge and milk.

'Now,' she said, 'you sit by the fire and keep warm. I am going into the forest to get a bundle of sticks for the fire.'

And she wrapped a shawl round her head, took a piece of rope to tie the firewood together, and went out into the snow.

My word, it was cold! The snow was falling round her in big flakes, and she was soon white from head to foot It wasn't easy to find firewood, either, for everything was hidden under the snow, But she got a bundle of sticks at last, tied the bundle together with the rope, swung the bundle over her shoulder and turned to go home.

Then what should she see lying under a bush but a little sick kitten. The kitten was all white, except for a black streak between its eyes; its bones were sticking out, and it was dreadfully thin and ill.

'Oh, you poor little thing!' said the

woman. And she picked up the kitten, wrapped it in her apron, and carried it home.

When she got near home, the children came running to meet her. They were laughing and shouting and throwing snow-balls at each other. They saw that their mother was carrying something in her apron and they cried out, 'Oh, what have you got?'

'A poor little sick kitten,' said the woman.

'Let me have it to play with!' cried the little boy.

'No, let *me* have it!' cried the little girl.

But the woman said, 'No, it's too ill. You mustn't touch it – you will make it worse. When it gets better you shall play with it.'

She carried the kitten into the kitchen, laid it on an old cushion in front of the fire, and gave it some warm milk, opening its little mouth and dripping the milk in with a spoon, because the kitten was too ill to lap.

Well, the kitten soon got better, and then the woman said to the children, '*Now* you can play with it.' And fine romps they had, with a ball, and some cotton-reels, and such like. And all the time the kitten was growing, until there it was – a fine big cat, with the loveliest furry coat, all white, except for the one black streak between its eyes. It still slept on the old cushion in front of the kitchen fire; and one evening, before she went to bed, the little girl said, 'Goodnight, pussy dear.' And she picked up the cat and kissed in on the black streak between its eyes.

Next morning the cat had disappeared. They searched and searched. No, they couldn't find it anywhere. The children cried, but their mother said, 'You mustn't grieve, I expect it has gone back into the forest where it was born.'

The children ran into the forest to look for it; but they never found it. And by and by they gave up grieving.

One day in early summer the woman went again into the forest to gather sticks. The sun was shining, and the birds were singing. And when she had gathered her sticks, and made a bundle of them, and was turning to go home, she passed by the bush where she had first found the kitten. And there, standing beside the bush, was the most lovely lady.

The lady was dressed in white, and she wore a black ribbon in her hair. She was smiling.

'Don't you recognize me?' she said.

'No, my lady,' said the woman. 'I can't say I do.'

'I am your kitten,' said the lady. 'A wicked witch cast a spell on me. But when your little girl kissed me on the black streak between my eyes, she broke the spell. . . .

And here is something for you,' said she.

And she gave the woman five knitting-needles.

'Put these on the kitchen table before you go to bed. And now goodbye.'

Then the lovely lady waved her hand, and walked off among the trees. And the woman went home.

That evening the woman put the knitting-needles on the kitchen table, though she couldn't really see what use there was in that. But in the morning – what did she find on the table? A beautiful pair of knitted stockings.

'Oh,' said she, 'that's just what I need!'

She put on the stockings, and they fitted her exactly.

Next night she put the knitting-needles on the table again; and in the morning there was another pair of stockings – just the right size for the little girl. So, for the third time, the woman left the needles on the table overnight; and in the morning found a pair of stockings for the little boy.

So it went on: the woman leaving the needles on the table overnight, and in the morning finding yet another pair of stockings; until she and the children had just as many stockings as ever they could want. But the needles didn't stop knitting because of that. As long as the woman left those needles on the table overnight, so in the morning she found a new pair of stockings, some of fine, fine silk, some of soft warm wool, and of many different colours.

She took the stockings into town and sold them. Everyone was eager to buy such beautiful stockings; so she earned enough money to keep her and the children in comfort for the rest of their lives.

And every night, before she got into bed, the woman blessed and thanked the lovely lady who had so rewarded her. But she never saw that lovely lady again.

10 · Snail walking

A snail was out walking one day and he came to a bridge over a little river. He thought he would like to see what was on the other side of the river, so he stepped on the bridge. He went, went, went. It took him seven years to cross over that bridge; and just as he got safely to the other side of the river, the bridge broke and fell into the water.

'There!' said he. 'What a good thing that I'm a quick walker. If I hadn't been a quick walker I should have been drowned!'

11 · Snail and Wolf

Snail was taking a stroll. He looked down the road and saw Wolf hurrying along.

Snail said, 'Wolf, Wolf, where are you going?'

Wolf said, 'I'm going to Rome. And where do you think you're going?'

Snail said, 'Oh, I'm going to Rome, too.'

Wolf said, '*You* go to Rome! The lambs that are born today will have grown into horned rams before *you* get half-way there!'

Snail said, 'I bet I'll get to Rome before you do.'

Wolf said, 'Ha! Ha! What will you bet!'

Snail said, 'The price of a breakfast in Rome's best eating-house.'

Wolf said, 'Done!'

Then Snail made a line across the road and said, 'This is the starting point. I'll stand on the line, you'll put your hind feet on it. And when I say "Go!" we'll be off.'

'Ha! Ha!' Wolf put his hind feet on the

line. What did Snail do? All unknown to Wolf, he climbed up on to Wolf's tail. Then he called out 'Go!'

Wolf galloped off. Snail sat smiling on Wolf's tail. He was having a fine ride.

It was a long way to Rome. Wolf was running all day. When he got to Rome it was evening, and the gate into the city was closed. So Wolf sat down outside the gate to wait for morning. And soon he fell asleep.

Then what did Snail do? He got off Wolf's tail, and crawled in under the gate. Yes, he was in Rome before Wolf! He spent an hour or two climbing up the inside of the gate; and when he got to the top he sat there laughing.

When Wolf woke, the sun was rising, but the gate was still closed.

'Hello there, Wolf! Hello there, Slow Coach!'

Who was that calling? Wolf looked up. What did he see? Snail peering down at him from the top of the gate.

'Ha!' said Snail. 'Here you are at last! I arrived in the city yesterday. Don't forget you owe me a breakfast. I've been waiting long enough for that breakfast!'

12 · The turnip

There was a little old woman and she sowed a whole handful of turnip seed in one small hole.

Soon there grew from all this seed just one turnip. And the turnip grew bigger, and *bigger*, and BIGGER.

'Now I will make me some nice turnip soup!' said the little old woman. And she took hold of the turnip to pull it up out of the ground.

She pulled and pulled. But she couldn't pull up that turnip. So she went to look for someone to help her, and she met Firstly.

'Firstly,' said she, 'come and help me to pull up my turnip. And when we've got it out of the ground, I'll give you a pot full of it.'

Firstly came. He caught hold of the little old woman round the waist. The little old woman caught hold of the turnip. They pulled and pulled. But they couldn't pull up that turnip.

Then away went the little old woman and met Secondly.

'Secondly, come and help to pull up my

turnip. When we've pulled it up, I'll give you a pot full of it.'

Secondly came. He caught hold of Firstly. Firstly caught hold of the little old woman. The little old woman caught hold of the turnip. They pulled and pulled, but they couldn't pull it up.

So away went the little old woman again and met Thirdly.

'Thirdly, come and help me to pull up my turnip. When we have pulled it up, I'll give you a pot full of it.'

Thirdly came. He caught hold of Secondly. Secondly caught hold of Firstly, Firstly caught hold of the little old woman, the little old woman caught hold of the turnip. They all pulled and pulled. Could they pull up that turnip? No, they couldn't.

So away went the little old woman and met Fourthly.

'Fourthly, come and help me pull up my turnip.'

Fourthly came. He caught hold of Thirdly. Thirdly caught hold of Secondly, Secondly caught hold of Firstly, Firstly caught hold of the little old woman, the little old woman caught hold of the turnip. They pulled and pulled. But they couldn't pull up that turnip.

So it went on. The little old woman fetched Fifthly, Sixthly, Seventhly, Eighthly, Ninthly. They caught hold of each other, and the little old woman caught hold of the turnip. They all pulled and pulled. But they couldn't pull it up.

So then the little old woman fetched Tenthly.

'Tenthly, come and help me to pull up my turnip. When we have pulled it up I will give you a pot full of it.'

Tenthly came.

He caught hold of Ninthly.

Ninthly caught hold of Eighthly.

Eighthly caught hold of Seventhly.

Seventhly caught hold of Sixthly.

Sixthly caught hold of Fifthly.

Fifthly caught hold of Fourthly.

Fourthly caught hold of Thirdly.

Thirdly caught hold of Secondly.

Secondly caught hold of Firstly.

Firstly caught hold of the little old woman.

The little old woman caught hold of the turnip.

They pulled, *pulled*, *pulled*, *PULLED* – And up came the turnip. It came up with such a jerk that the little old woman fell back on top of Firstly, Firstly fell back on top of Secondly, Secondly fell back on top of Thirdly, Thirdly fell back on top of Fourthly, Fourthly fell back on top of Fifthly, Fifthly fell back on top of Sixthly, Sixthly fell back on top of Seventhly, Seventhly fell back on top of Eighthly, Eighthly fell back on top of Ninthly, Ninthly fell back on top of Tenthly, Tenthly fell to the ground.

All in a heap they rolled, one on top of the other. And while they were picking themselves up, the turnip ran off laughing.

13 · Old Man and the rock

Once upon a time Old Man was going on his travels to see the world. He walked along and he walked along till he tired himself out, and he sat down on a rock to rest awhile. Then after he had rested, he got up to travel on, and the sun was blazing hot. So he took off his overcoat, laid it on the rock and said, 'Rock, I give you my coat because you are poor, and because you have let me rest. You may keep my coat for always.'

Then he walked on. But he hadn't gone far when it began to rain, and he met

Rabbit, and said, 'Little brother Rabbit,
run back to the rock and ask him for my
overcoat. We will cover ourselves with it
and keep dry.'

Rabbit ran to the rock. Very soon he
came running back again, but he wasn't
bringing the overcoat.

Old Man said, 'Where's my coat?'

Rabbit said, 'The rock wouldn't give it
to me. He said you had made him a present
of it, and he was going to keep it.'

Then Old Man was angry. He went to the rock himself, snatched the coat, and said, 'I only wanted to borrow it until it stopped raining; then I would have given it back to you. But now, since you are so unmannerly, I shall keep it. What do you want with an overcoat anyway? You have spent your whole life out in the rain and snow. It won't hurt you to go on living in the same way now.'

Old Man went back with the coat to Rabbit, and they found a little hollow between two banks, and sat down there. They covered themselves up with the coat, and Old Man said, 'Now it can rain as hard as it likes; we are very snug and comfortable.'

So they sat there, and it went on raining. But by and by they heard a loud noise, *Boom – bump! Boom – bump!* And Old Man said, 'Little brother Rabbit, creep up on to the bank, and see what that noise is.'

Rabbit crept up to the top of the bank, and came bounding back before you could count three, crying out, 'Run! Run! The rock is coming!'

Then they both ran away as fast as they could, and the rock was coming after them, *Boom – bump! Boom – bump!* Old Man was very frightened; he threw off his overcoat and shouted, 'Take it, rock!' But rock came on, *Boom – bump! Boom – bump!* So Old Man threw off all his clothes, first one and then another, and flung them behind him, shouting, 'Take them, rock! Take them, rock!' But still the rock came on – *Boom – bump! Boom – bump!* And it was coming closer and closer.

Then Old Man saw a herd of buffaloes and cried to them, 'Help me, help me, brothers! Stop that rock!'

The buffaloes came galloping, heads down, and charged the rock. But all they did, poor things, was to flatten their foreheads against it. And they have had flat foreheads ever since. So Old Man ran on, and Rabbit ran on, and there was the rock still coming after them, *Boom – bump! Boom – bump!*

Then a company of rattlesnakes came out of a wood to see what was going on, and Old Man cried to them, 'Help me, help me, brothers! Stop that rock!'

The rattlesnakes twined themselves together into a noose and flung themselves round the rock; but the rock burst through the noose, and came on, *Boom – bump! Boom – bump!* Now it was so near Old Man that it was bumping against his heels, and Old Man looked up and saw a flock of big birds, and cried out, 'Help me, brothers! Help me, I am almost killed! Stop that rock!'

The big birds swooped down. They swooped down one after the other, and struck the rock with their beaks. And every time one of them struck against it, he broke off a piece of the rock with his beak. And at last one bird struck the rock exactly in the centre, and it broke into two pieces. So where it was it had to stay. It couldn't run any more.

Old Man flopped down beside the broken rock. He couldn't run another step.

The birds flew away, and Old Man called after them, 'Thank you, thank you, my brothers! When I can do you a good turn, I will; but now I must sleep. . . . And you, friend Rabbit, just stand beside me

and keep watch. . . . Wake me if any danger threatens. . . .'

Old Man yawned, and shut his eyes. Soon he was snoring.

But Rabbit ran off. No, Old Man wasn't the kind of friend he liked.

14 · The letter in the egg

There was once a lovely garden,
Here a garden, there a garden,
Wasn't that a lovely garden!

In the garden was a tree,
Here a tree, there a tree,
Wasn't that a lovely tree!

In the tree there was a nest,
Here a nest, there a nest,
Wasn't that a lovely nest!

In the nest there was a bird,
Here a bird, there a bird,
Wasn't that a lovely bird!

In the bird there was an egg,
Here an egg, there an egg,
Wasn't that a lovely egg!

In the egg there was a yolk,
Here a yolk, there a yolk,
Wasn't that a lovely yolk!

In the yolk there was a letter,
Here a letter, there a letter,
Wasn't that a lovely letter!

In the letter it stands written
'All good children love each other'!

You can see more Methuen Paperbacks on the
following pages.

*For more information about the latest Methuen
Paperbacks, for both adults and children, write to:*

Methuen Paperbacks
North Way
Andover
Hampshire SP10 5BE
England

MABEL ESTHER ALLAN

The Wood Street Group
The Wood Street Helpers
The Wood Street Rivals
The Wood Street Secret

A series of exciting adventures about the Wood
Street Group – a lively gang of children – set
against an authentic Liverpool background.

Illustrated by Shirley Hughes

Nonsense verse *selected by* **WILLIAM COLE**

Oh What Nonsense!
Oh That's Ridiculous!
Beastly Boys and Ghastly Girls
Oh How Silly!

Each book has a selection of funny, absurd and truly
ridiculous rhymes accompanied by hilarious
drawings – guaranteed to make you giggle!

Illustrated by Tomi Ungerer